Dream Station

Anthony Ram

First Edition

PAGE PUBLISHING, INC.
Conneaut Lake, PA

First originally published by Page Publishing 2020

ISBN 978-1-64334-860-5 (pbk)
ISBN 978-1-64334-857-5 (digital)

Printed in the United States of America

CHAPTER 1

MORNING ROUTINE

Today was an ordinary day like any other for Jordan Jenson. The skies outside were a little overcast, dreary, and mug. He could hear his mom downstairs making lunches, which consisted of the usual peanut butter and jelly with no crust, a bag of chips, and bottle of water, and since today was Tuesday, there would be apple slices instead of an orange. As for Jordan's dad, he was more than likely running late for work and looking frantically for his keys that were probably in his pants that he wore the day before. Jordan's parents were both very into their careers. Jordan's mom was an attorney who was always working on some big case that was confidential, and Jordan's dad also had a demanding job saving lives as a trauma doctor. This meant there wasn't much time for Jordan.

Jordan lay in his room dreading getting out of bed for another day of school. He sat up, stretched, and looked out the window past the little pirate ship in the glass bottle that sat on the dresser, hoping that today would be better than the last.

A couple of seconds later, Jordan's mom called up, "Jordan, it's time for school. Hurry up, or you're going to be late again."

Jordan replied, "Okay, Mom, be right down." Jordan climbed out of bed and walked toward his closet to try to find something to wear.

Jordan had a simple taste in clothes, usually a plain-colored shirt, a pair of jeans, and his favorite pair shoes that were given to him by his grandmother. After getting dressed, he walked to his bathroom. Jordan put the same tooth-whitening toothpaste on his toothbrush that he has used his whole life and started to brush. After brushing his teeth, he washed his mouth out with the tingly mouthwash that he hated but knew was important. Jordan had a thing for being clean and smelling fresh. He hated to be dirty. Again, Jordan could hear his mom yelling from downstairs, "Jordan, we're leaving for work. Your lunch is on the counter, and your waffles are in the toaster. Have a good day. Love you." Before Jordan could reply, he heard the front door shut, and he could hear both their cars start. Jordan whispered to himself under his breath, "Love you too," and continued with his morning routine. Now that he was done with his teeth, he combed his hair the same way he had been combing it since the third grade and went downstairs to sit down for breakfast.

Jordan grabbed the two waffles from the toaster and put them in the trash and headed for the fridge. One thing that Jordan loved to do that no one knew was he loved to cook. Jordan loved being able to take different ingredients and create something special. Jordan looked in the fridge wondering what he would make today. He reached for the eggs, bell peppers, onions, and a few more ingredients. Jordan decided that for breakfast today, he was going to make a country omelet. He turned on the stove got out the pans and placed all the ingredients on the counter. He tossed in some butter in the pan to let it melt. As the butter began to sizzle, Jordan cracked the eggs into a bowl, stirred them up, and poured them into the pan. Jordan loved the feeling of creating something with his own two hands. He diced up some ham, red bell peppers, and some onion and added that to the pan. Jordan thought to himself, *Here comes the hard part, flipping the eggs over into a perfect omelet.* He used the spatula and flipped the eggs perfectly. As he waited for the eggs to cook, he set the table wishing he could set two more places for his parents, but they were always so busy. Jordan's omelet was finished, and he poured a glass of orange juice and sat down to try his creation. "*Mmm,* this is great. Best one yet."

As Jordan was cleaning up the kitchen, he heard the door open and then he heard, "*Jordan,* what's up bro?" Jordan knew it could only be one person, his best and only friend, Nico. Nico and Jordan had lived next door to each other since they were in diapers, and they have been inseparable. Nico was pretty much the coolest kid at their middle school. He was great at every sport and was always able to make everyone laugh. Nico was a year older than Jordan, so they weren't in the same grade. That made it hard for them to hang out at school, but every morning, they would walk there together since they only lived a few blocks away.

"Hey, man, are you ready to go?"

"Yeah, just let me grab my backpack." Jordan grabbed his backpack, and they headed out the door. As Jordan locked the door, he heard Nico say something.

"Hey, bro, did you watch the game last night?"

"No, I missed it. I had to finish a report for Mrs. Sike's history class."

"Oh man, it was insane. It came down to three seconds left on the clock, and Wilson stepped back and threw a deep pass into the end zone for the win!" Nico was all about football and had the dream to play professionally one day.

Jordan and Nico continued to talk as they walked to school but then everything got silent as Jordan looked up, and out of the corner of his eye, he caught a glimpse of his childhood crush, Terra Simpson. Terra was class president and captain of the volleyball team.

"Hello. Hello. Jordan, close your mouth. You're drooling." Nico snapped Jordan back to reality.

"Sorry, man, I must have zoned out."

Nico knew that Jordan had a huge crush on Terra, and he always encouraged Jordan to just talk to her, but Jordan was so scared that he would say something dumb and mess up. As Jordan and Nico got to school, the bell rang, and they went their separate ways.

CHAPTER 2

LIFE AT SCHOOL

Jordan always dreaded going to his first class because it was PE. Jordan wasn't the most athletic kid, but he wasn't the worst either. The reason why Jordan worried about going to PE was Marcus Johnson. Marcus was a big loudmouthed kid that always picked on Jordan. Any chance Marcus got, he would call Jordan names, push him around when the teachers weren't looking, and try to embarrass Jordan in front of the class. One time in fourth grade, Marcus spat a huge wad of gum into Jordan's hair, and it was so bad that Jordan had to shave his head to get it all out.

Jordan got changed into his PE clothes and was on his way out of the locker room and headed to the basketball courts. As he turned the corner, Marcus tripped him, and Jordan fell right on his face, and the whole class laughed. A couple of seconds later, Coach Johnson walked out. "All right. That's enough. Everybody, line up." Jordan hopped up, dusted himself off, and got in line like nothing happened because he knew if he let Marcus see him hurt, he would win.

"All right, class. Today, we're going to be playing basketball." Jordan was actually a little excited about this because basketball was something that he enjoyed. "All right, we're going to split into four teams of five, two teams on this court and two teams on that court." Jordan was praying that he would be on a different court than Marcus, but with his luck, there was no chance.

Of course, they were on the same court but different teams. As they began to play, Jordan tried to keep his distance from Marcus but knew something was bound to happen. Things were going well, and his plan of staying away from Marcus was working until Jordan got the ball, and Marcus was guarding him. Jordan decided to try to shoot, and as he jumped to shoot the ball, Marcus pulled down Jordan's pants, and the whole class laughed. Jordan frantically tried to pull up his shorts and finally managed to do so, but he was so embarrassed. Jordan stood there with a red face. A second later, you could hear Coach Johnson, "Marcus, apologize right now and then get yourself to the principal's office." All that Jordan could think was at least this time, Marcus was caught by Coach Johnson and would get punished.

Coach Johnson pulled Jordan aside. "Are you all right, Jordan? Do you need anything, or want to head to the locker room a little early?"

"No, I'll be all right."

Jordan went back to playing basketball wanting to put it past him. When PE was over, Jordan was happy to be headed to his next class, and hopefully, the day will get better but that wasn't Jordan's luck. Jordan sat down for math, and he heard little laughing behind him. At first, he didn't think anything of it, but then one of the kids in his class said, "Nice underwear, Jordan!" When Jordan was pantsed during PE, someone snapped a picture, and now it's going around the whole school. Jordan was so embarrassed and just wanted to crawl into a little hole and never come out. The rest of the class, Jordan buried his head in his book and waited for it to be over.

Finally, math was over, and it was time for lunch. Jordan was so happy for lunch because Nico and Jordan had the same lunch, and he wasn't alone. Nico was waiting for Jordan at his locker, and he heard what happened and felt bad, but Nico had a way to fix it. Nico thought it would be best not to mention the incident. He just said, "Hey, man, let's head to the cafeteria and get some lunch." They walked to their usual table, but as they walked, everyone started to laugh. While people were laughing, Nico got up on the table, and everyone got quiet. "You guys think underpants are so funny." Right then, he pantsed himself, and everyone stopped laughing. Nico pulled up his pants and said, "Look, now you being pantsed at PE is old news."

Jordan realized how lucky he was to have a friend like Nico. Jordan always wondered why one of the coolest kids in school would hang out with him and stick up for him beyond what any other friend would do. Everybody went about their business, and Jordan and Nico went on to eat their lunch and chat about the same stuff like always.

The last half of his day wasn't so bad, and he was headed to his favorite class next, science. The reason Jordan loved science so much was because it was similar to cooking. With science much like cooking, Jordan is able to explore and create things out of nothing. Today, they were working on chemistry and compounds and what they do when mixed together. Another thing that Jordan liked about science was his teacher Mrs. Robinson. Mrs. Robinson always made Jordan feel at ease when he entered her class because he knew that he wouldn't get picked on, or teased because Mrs. Robinson hated bullying.

The bell rang. "All right, class, take your seats. We're going to get started. Today, we are going to be working with specific chemicals, and you will need to choose a partner. Everyone, make sure to put on your safety glasses, gloves, and aprons." Jordan usually waited to pair up with the other person that didn't have a partner, but this time, there was an extra. Today, there was an odd amount because someone was absent, which was okay because Jordan preferred to work alone.

As he was starting to read the board and figure out, which chemicals to mix to create a solution, the classroom door opened. Jordan looked toward the door and he noticed it was Terra.

"Hi, Mrs. Robinson. Sorry, I'm late. I had a dentist appointment." Mrs. Robinson looked at the note.

"Not a problem, Terra. Grab some goggles, gloves, and an apron. And it looks like you're going to be partnered with Jordan."

This was Jordan's dream come true but also his biggest nightmare. "Hi, I'm Terra. Looks like we're going to be working together today." Jordan tried to talk, but he couldn't think of what to say because he was still in shock that he was working with Terra Simpson. Finally, he was able to respond and all that came out was "*Hmm.*" Terra just smiled back at Jordan.

Terra took at the board and processed the chemicals. "All right, so from the chemicals that are on the board, it looks like we're recreating the Briggs-Rauscher reaction." All that Jordan could think to himself was, *How did she know that?* Again, all Jordan could say was, "*Hmm.*" Then Terra whispered to Jordan, "Don't tell anyone, but I'm kind of a science nerd." Terra grabbed the chemicals that were on the board, which were potassium iodate, sulfuric acid, and water to make the first solution. As she mixed the first chemicals together, she asked Jordan if he was a fan of science. This time, Jordan was able to respond with more than *hmm*. "Yes, I actually am really into science too!" While she mixed the chemicals for the first solution, Jordan started on the next solution. The next solution was made up of malonic acid, manganese sulfate monohydrate, and water. When they each finished their solutions, they started to work on the last solution together. The last solution was made of just hydrogen peroxide and water. Now that they had all their solutions created, they were going to mix them all together and see what happens.

Jordan and Terra poured all the solutions into the large glass and waited to see what happened. The colors started to change, and the water started to spiral in a tornado shape in the glass. "This is so cool! This is the best experiment that we have done so far!" Jordan was so surprised to see how much Terra enjoyed science and started to like her even more. Jordan realized that they had more in common than he thought.

Mrs. Robinson tapped her glasses on the desk. "All right, class, the bell is about to ring in a few minutes, so let's clean up our stations." As Jordan and Terra started to clean up, Terra asked Jordan why she never sees him around school, or at any of the games, or school events. Jordan explained to her that he wasn't really into those kind of things and preferred to hang out at his house. Jordan didn't want to tell her it was because he was afraid that he would run into Marcus, and he didn't want that. Terra grabbed her backpack and headed for the door.

"Well, Jordan, maybe I'll see you around more often."

Jordan looked up. "Yeah, I hope so. I had a really fun time working with you."

Terra smiled back. "Have a nice day. See you around, Jordan."

Jordan headed to his last class of the day, which was home economics. Jordan liked this class, but he was kind of limited because he had to cook to the specifications of the teacher, and his creativity was limited. Jordan got to class and sat down at his table with his cooking partner, but his partner was absent today. His teacher, Mrs. Jasper, tapped her wooden spoon against the board. "All right, boys and girls we're going to be making mini chocolate cakes today. Go ahead and grab your ingredients and get to baking following the instructions on the board. Oh, and before I forget, Jordan, your partner, Josh, transferred to woodshop, and we will be getting another student for you tomorrow, so for today, you are on your own." Jordan nodded his head. Jordan wasn't really a fan of following directions when cooking, but at least he got to make something and do what he enjoys.

Jordan followed the directions on the board and made his chocolate cake. Once the cake was finished baking, he pulled it out of the oven and let it cool. Once it was cool enough, he was able to put on the icing. Jordan thought it looked pretty good. He took a bite, and it was rather tasty, but he thought to himself that he could probably make something better by himself. Jordan cleaned up his station and waited for the bell to ring so he could go home.

CHAPTER 3

REVENGE OF THE BULLY

Now that the day was over, Jordan started to walk home by himself because Nico had basketball practice after school. Jordan wished at times that Nico didn't have practice so they could hang out more, especially on a day like today because he wanted so badly to tell Nico about being partners with Terra in science. As Jordan was walking up to the street that his house was on, Marcus walked out from behind a tree. Marcus had been waiting for Jordan to get out of school so he could catch him walking home. "Hey, nerd, because of you, I got Saturday school for the next three weeks!" Jordan was in shock and didn't know what to do. He tried to run, but his body was frozen, like a deer in the headlights. "Now you're gonna pay for it." Marcus shoved Jordan to the ground and pushed his face into the grass. Jordan tried to mumble through the dirt. "I'm sorry. I didn't mean for you to get in trouble." Marcus grabbed Jordan's backpack and ripped up his notebooks and threw them on the ground. "You're lucky I don't beat you worse for what you did, nerd." Marcus kicked Jordan's backpack and walked away. Jordan wiped the tears from his eyes, grabbed his stuff that was scattered on the sidewalk, and went into his house.

"Why? Why does he have to pick on me?" Jordan wished that he could figure out why Marcus chose to pick on only him. Had he done something to make him mad, or make him feel upset in the past, but Jordan couldn't think of anything. As he washed the mud from his face, he wished that he had someone to talk and get advice from. Jordan didn't like to tell Nico when this kind of stuff happened because he knew Nico would do something that might get him in trouble. Jordan couldn't talk to his parents about his problems because they came home really late. After they did get home, they still were busy, working late into the night until they were so exhausted, and all they would want is to crawl into bed. After Jordan got all the mud from his face, he headed to his room to start on his homework. It usually only took Jordan an hour to finish all his homework. He always liked to get that out of the way first so that he could do what he loved before his parents got home.

Jordan finished his homework, closed his laptop, and began heading down stairs. He figured being in the kitchen would help him forget about Marcus. He got to the kitchen and looked in the fridge for what he was going to create tonight. Jordan was thinking of making something Italian. He made sure all the ingredients were there because tonight he was feeling in the mood for a chicken Fettuccine Alfredo.

First things first! Jordan grabbed all the ingredients from the fridge and pantry and placed them on the counter. He turned on the oven, and as the gas clicked and the flames came through, Jordan's eyes lit up as bright as the flames. All the worries and bad things that happened that day disappeared. Jordan began by cleaning and dicing the chicken. Next he put the pot of water on the stove and waited for it to boil so he could pour in the pasta. Just as he was about to dice the broccoli, he heard a noise at the front door. The door was locked, so it couldn't be Nico. He heard, "Hey, Jordan, I'm home early." It was Jordan's mom. "I picked up a pizza. Hope you're hungry."

Jordan couldn't believe it. He didn't like people to know about his secret love for cooking, and now his mom was about to find out. Jordan's mom walked into kitchen and looked at everything that was going on, and she was shocked.

"Jordan, what are you doing with all this food?"

"Um, I was making chicken fettucine." Jordan's mom wasn't upset. She was just surprised to see Jordan in the kitchen.

"Well, it smells amazing!"

"You're not mad, Mom?"

"No, I'm a little nervous about the knives and the stove, but it actually looks like you know what you're doing. Where did you learn to cook like this?" Jordan didn't really read cookbooks, or watch cooking shows. He just liked to mix ingredients and try things that he had seen, or tasted in restaurants when he would go out with his parents.

"I remember trying this pasta before at a restaurant, and it's one of my favorites, so I thought I would make it for dinner tonight."

"That explains why we always have so many freezer meals, and the fresh produce is always gone."

Jordan's mom got up from the counter and gave Jordan a hug. "Well, I am going to put my stuff away and change out of these clothes and then I'll be back to give you a hand." Jordan was relieved that his mom wasn't mad and that she was actually going to spend some time with him. Jordan picked back up where he left off and starting dicing up the broccoli to add for the pasta. Jordan checked on the chicken, and it was looking good. And now that the noodles were finished, he could combine the chicken and noodles into the same pot.

"All right, I'm back. Is there anything I can help you with?"

"Um, you can get out the mozzarella and parmesan cheeses, some milk, and whipping cream." Jordan's mom grabbed the ingredients and handed them to Jordan so he could add them to the pasta.

They were working well together, then Jordan's mom asked how his day at school was. Jordan didn't want to tell her about how he got bullied, so he just said, "Things were good. Just another day. Nothing too eventful."

"That's good. How are your grades?"

"They're good. I'm pretty sure I still have all As. How was work for you?"

"It was not too bad. My court case got postponed so that is why I came home early."

Jordan was almost finished, just adding the final touches with some garlic salt, pepper, and a little parsley for garnish. Jordan gave it a little taste. "Mmm." It had turned out better than he has ever made it before. Now that it was all done, Jordan grabbed some plates while his mom got the drinks, and they sat down for dinner.

Jordan thought to himself, *This was going to be interesting since they never really sat down together alone just the two of them.* As they sat down to eat, Jordan's mom tried the fettuccine and was amazed at Jordan's cooking ability.

"Jordan, this is wonderful, and I'm not just saying that because I'm your mother."

"Thanks!" Jordan had a little grin on his face because he never has had anyone try his food, and he was glad his mom was the first.

"I'm going to make an effort to come home from work earlier so that we can spend time in the kitchen together."

Jordan liked the sound of that but knew that it was more than likely not going to happen because his mom was so busy, but he hoped maybe this time it was true.

CHAPTER 4

NEWS FROM MOM

"That was delicious, Jordan. How about we clean up, and if you want, I think we have a little time before it gets too late, we can grab some ice cream from Velvets Ice Cream Parlor."

"That would be great, Mom!"

They started cleaning the dishes and putting things away, and when they were finished, Jordan and his mom headed for the car. Jordan was so happy to be getting ice cream with his mom at his favorite ice cream parlor. Just then, Jordan started to think, *This is too good to be true.* First, his mom came home with pizza. Now, she's taking him to get ice cream. She never does this kind of stuff now, and out of nowhere, she is making time. Something must be up.

As they sat in the car listening to country music playing softly, Jordan asked his mom, "Is something wrong?" It got real quiet, and it took her a couple of seconds to respond.

"Nothing gets by you, does it, Jordan?" Jordan's mom took a deep breath and told Jordan that she and his father were getting divorced. Jordan didn't know what to say, or how he should feel.

Jordan and his parents hardly spent time together anyway, so it wasn't that hard for him.

"Okay, Mom, I understand."

"Jordan, I want you to know that it is not your fault your father and I have just grown apart. We both love you very much and are not doing this to hurt you." Jordan started to think of how this was going to affect him and would he be moving, or would they sell the house and would he have to live in two different places, or choose between his mom and dad. Jordan and his mom arrived at the ice cream shop. "Let's go in and grab a pint of your favorite ice cream, and we can talk about it, and I can answer all the questions you need while we work our way to the bottom of the carton."

"Okay, Mom."

As Jordan stood in line with his mom to get the ice cream, he was trying to think of all the questions that he was going to ask and wanted to start with the big ones. The only problem was the only thing he could think about at that moment was how this whole thing ruined his favorite ice cream shop! From now on, every time he goes there, it will remind him of his parents getting divorced. It was their turn to buy the ice cream, and the cashier was Albert who knew Jordan very well because he was in there at least once a week.

"Hey, Jordan, how's it going? Come in for an after-dinner craving of double fudge brownie?" Which was Jordan's favorite.

In a soft tone, Jordan answered, "Hey, Albert. Yeah, me and my mom are going to split it tonight." Albert could tell by the tone in his voice that something was wrong but figured it best not to say anything in front of his mom.

"All right. Well, you two enjoy the ice cream, and I'll see you sometime next week, Jordan."

"Thanks, Albert. See ya later."

Jordan and his mom got back in the car and headed home. The car ride home was a little awkward, good thing they only lived a few minutes away. As they pulled into the garage, Jordan noticed that his dad's car wasn't in the driveway. It was past nine, and his dad was usually home around then, so he wondered where he could be.

"All right, Jordan. I'm going to run on up and scoop the ice cream into a couple bowls for us and put the rest in the freezer before it melts. Can you please pull out the trash cans?"

"Okay."

Jordan's mom went into the house and scooped the ice cream while Jordan pulled out the cans. As Jordan went out to the curb to grab the cans, he paused and looked up at the moon and wished that this whole day never happened.

Jordan closed the garage and slowly walked into the kitchen to what he knew would be one of the most awkward moments of his life.

"Hey, honey, here's your ice cream. Want to sit on the couch and talk about some stuff?"

"Sure, Mom."

As Jordan sank into the couch, he thought of where he would start. Before he could think, he blurted out, "Are we going to have to sell the house and move?"

"Calm down, Jordan. It's all right. We are not going to move. Your father and I decided that it would be best for you to stay here and at your school and close to your friends since this will be a tough transition." All Jordan could think of was how much of a relief it would be to not have to switch schools and move to a new place where he knew no one.

"Your dad got an apartment downtown and is going to be living there from now on."

"So how will time be split?"

"That's a good question. Your dad and I figured that you would spend weeks here with me and every other weekend with him if that sounds okay to you?" Jordan was actually kind of happy with that since he never really saw his dad anyway, it wouldn't be much of a change.

"Sure, Mom. That should be fine."

"I'm so sorry that you have to go through this, Jordan. I can't imagine how you must be feeling. It's late. Why don't you head on upstairs and get some rest." Jordan slowly slumped up the stairs after what had to be the longest day of his life.

Finally in his room, all Jordan could think about was taking a shower and trying to wash the day away, then crawl into bed. Jordan turned on the water and let the room heat up until the steam covered the whole bathroom, and he could barely see. As he stepped into the shower, he did think of the silver lining of that day was that he was able to share his love for cooking with his mom. Jordan stood in the steam-filled shower and continued to think of how nice it would be if he could share his love of cooking with the world and not have the fear being made fun of and being called names like Betty Crocker. Now that he was done washing up, he turned off the light and crawled into bed.

Jordan lay there in his bed like he did this morning staring out the window past the ship in the bottle at the starry night sky. He wished that he could be anywhere else than where he was now, somewhere he could forget all that's going on in his life and just relax. He knew that was never going to happen because he was just a twelve-year-old kid, and this was not a movie. This was real life. Jordan adjusted the pillows, lay back, and closed his eyes in hopes that tomorrow would be better day than today.

CHAPTER 5

CRAZY DREAM

Jordan was fast asleep, but he felt like he could hear something, something that he never heard before. It was a slight rumbling but then it started to get louder and louder like heard of elephant running in the jungle. Then all at once, it came to an abrupt halt. Then all of a sudden, he heard an ear-ringing whistle. Jordan went over to the window and looked out. What he saw was a train that was black as coal stopped right in front of his house. Jordan rubbed his eyes in disbelief and looked again, but there the train was.

Jordan grabbed his slippers and went downstairs, opened the door, and peaked outside. Things kept getting stranger. Now not only was there a train parked in the front of his house with no sight of any train tracks, Jordan was able to get a look at the conductor, and it was his science teacher, Mrs. Robinson!

"Mrs. Robinson, is that you?"

"Yes, Jordan, it's me. I am here to take you to a very special place that I know you will love. It is your choice, Jordan, would you like to hop on and go to a place others only dream of, or would you rather stay here? *The choice is yours.*"

Jordan looked back at his house, and he didn't really want to think about what was going on there and looked at Mrs. Robinson. He decided that he was going to take a chance and get on the train. "All right, Jordan make sure to keep all hands and feet inside the train at all times. It's going to get a little bumpy."

Jordan could not believe that this was real! "Am I still dreaming? There's no way. This is to real." Jordan looked out the window as the train started up. Mrs. Robinson yelled back from the front of the train, "Hold on, Jordan. Takeoffs are a little rough." Jordan took a seat and waited for the train to move, but then all of a sudden, he felt a jolt.

The train didn't go forward or backward. It felt like it was going up. The train had lifted into the air! "*Here we go!*"

The train took off into the night sky, and Jordan was more scared than he has ever been in his entire life but at the same time felt somewhat excited. Over the loudspeaker, Jordan could hear Mrs. Robinson's voice. "We are now at a cruising altitude of thirty-five thousand feet. You are free to move about the train. We should be reaching our destination shortly!" Jordan got up walked to the front of the train to try to find out what was going on.

Jordan reached the front of the train and had a hundred questions for Mrs. Robinson, but the first question was, "Where are we heading?" As Jordan opened the door to the cabin where Mrs. Robinson was driving, he froze. Jordan caught a look outside and could see nothing but blue sky.

"Hey, Jordan, glad you came up. Have a seat. You can see out over all the states from up here." Jordan took a seat and began to clear his throat.

"Umm, Mrs. Robinson, where exactly are we headed?"

"Well, Jordan, it's kind of hard to explain. Where we're headed is not really on any map." Jordan had no clue on what to think with that response.

"Okay, Mrs. Robinson. But why am I the only one on this train?"

"Another good question, Jordan, but I can't answer that. I just drive the train and pick up the people that are on the manifest. Tonight, it had your name on it. Enough questions, Jordan. I'll need you to buckle up. We're going to be landing right there."

CHAPTER 6

PIRATE ISLAND

Jordan looked out the window and saw a small island in the middle of the vast ocean.

"We're going to land there?" screamed Jordan.

"Yep, so hold on. This could get a little bumpy."

Jordan strapped into the seat and held on for dear life. As the train landed and finally came to a stop, Jordan opened his eyes and took a look outside to make sure everything was all right. He looked out the window and saw a bunch of palm trees and waves crashing on a beautiful black sand beach.

Shouting at the top of her lungs, "Last stop. Everybody off!"

Jordan asked, "Where are we?"

"We are at your destination, of course: *Pirate Island.*"

Again, Jordan's mind was going a thousand miles per second trying to figure out what was going on. Jordan stepped off the train and onto the soft sand. Mrs. Robinson started the train and said, "All right, Jordan, I'll be back to get you by the end of the weekend. Before I forget, this is for you to help on your journey." She tossed a backpack onto the sand. Before Jordan could tell her to wait, she was gone. "What am I supposed to do here, and where is here?" Jordan took a second to catch his breath, and once he was calm, he grabbed the backpack and opened it up to see what was inside. The contents of the backpack contained a change of clothes, two water bottles, a pot, a knife, a space blanket, and two protein bars. Jordan double checked to see if there was anything else, and when he reached deep into the backpack, he felt a piece of paper. He pulled it out and looked at it. The piece of paper seemed to be some sort of a map and he wondered why that was in there. Jordan changed his clothes, packed everything else up in the backpack, and decided to take a look around.

Jordan walked along the beach and noticed some smoke coming from atop of the trees. He decided to head toward the smoke because it may be someone who has answers to why he was on the island. As he walked through the jungle, he wondered what if the person making the fire was not welcoming, then what would he do? He stopped to get a drink of water, so he removed his pack and grabbed the bottle. Jordan took one drink, and while he was drinking, he heard a noise. Jordan dropped the bottle and remembered that he had a knife. He reached for the knife and waited for whatever made that noise to do it again. A second later, he heard a bush moving again, and before he could turn around to see what it was, a pirate jumped out and grabbed him. Jordan screamed and then at least a half a dozen more jumped out while he was screaming.

Jordan dropped the knife as one of the pirates snatched him up by his backpack faster than you could say Pirate Island. Jordan's eyes were shut so tight, he could feel the pirate's hot breath against his face. Then Jordan heard a deep scratchy voice say, "What's a little boy like yourself doing on my side of the island? Did me rotten no-good brother send you here to spy on us?" Jordan could not say a single word because he was terrified for his life. "Well, go on. Out with it, boy." Jordan was barely able to get out the word No in a whisper voice. "What's that, boy? Speak up. I can't hear ya." Jordan tried again. This time, he was able to say it a little louder.

"No, sir." The pirate then put Jordan back on the ground.

"Well then, what are ya doin' here?"

"I'm not sure. A train dropped me off."

"A train. What's a train?" Jordan was baffled by that question.

"Umm, it's a like a big car that takes you from one location to another." As Jordan tried to explain what a train was, he could tell that the pirates had no idea what he was talking about. "It's not important." Jordan asked the pirate. "Do you know where I am?"

"Well, of course, boy. You're on Pirate Island. I'm Captain Joe Morley, and this is my crew. We're here looking for the buried treasure of Old Blue Beard."

Jordan could not believe what was going on. Just when he thought things couldn't get weirder than a flying train, he got taken by a band of pirates searching for buried treasure. All Jordan could think was if things are going to continue to get more and more strange.

"Excuse me, Mr. Captain Morley, but how long have you been on this island looking for the treasure?"

"There will be time for questions later, boy. We need to be gettin' back to camp before the sun goes down and the creatures of the night come out. Unless you would rather take your chances on yer own."

Jordan thought for a second as the pirates started to walk away and decided he would probably be a little safer with pirates then alone. Jordan ran after the pirates and followed close behind as they marched through the jungle.

While stomping through the jungle, Jordan noticed a bunch of odd-looking plants and a few animals that he had never seen even in books, or on television. One of the pirates whispered to Jordan, "Careful, boy, I know the plants look pretty, but get to close, and some can open up and swallow you whole." Jordan took a huge gulp and made sure to walk as careful as possible. *I wonder how far the camp is.* After walking for what seemed like forever, the pirates came to an abrupt stop. Jordan looked but did not see any camp. All of a sudden, Captain Morley made a sound like a dying bird, and a ladder came down from one of the trees high above their heads. Then a handful of other ladders rolled down, and the pirates began to climb up, disappearing behind the branches. Jordan followed with curiosity to see what was above. As Jordan reached the top, he looked around in amazement to see the most intricate tree house that he could ever imagine.

These pirates had a whole city in the trees. It was truly amazing. There were rooms for each of them to sleep, rooms where they kept their weapons, and it looked like a huge room for the kitchen and dining. Through all the commotion, Jordan realized he hadn't eaten anything all day, and he was starving. Jordan started to wonder what pirates liked to eat.

Then Jordan heard, "Aye, *boy*, get over here!" Jordan made his way over to Captain Morley. "This is where you'll be bunking till you find where you need to be goin'. While you're here, you're gonna have to pull your own weight. Got any skills?" Jordan took a second to think. He didn't want to tell them he liked to cook, but nothing else came to mind. Then Jordan was startled. "Well, boy, anything you think you can help with?"

Jordan blurted out, "I can cook." Then he covered his mouth with both hands as if he said a bad word in front of his mom.

"Well, well, we have a chef on our hands, do we? That's good, 'cause the chef we have now is terrible, so we'll give you a crack at it. Sound good, boy. You get to stay here if you cook for us."

Jordan replied, "Sure."

"All right then, we have a deal. Put your things away and go see Mr. Withers in the galley, and he'll show you around."

Jordan placed his backpack in his new room, sat on the bed, and took a look around. Jordan was so nervous. He has never cooked for anyone besides his mother. Now he was going to make dinner for more than twenty pirates. Jordan stood up, looked out the window, gave himself a little pep talk, and headed to meet Mr. Withers in the kitchen. As Jordan walked to the kitchen, the sun started to set, and through the trees and over the mountains, the light spread across the sky like he had never seen before.

Jordan reached the kitchen and went in to see who he assumed was Mr. Withers.

"Hello, Mr. Withers?"

"Ahoy, lad. Cap'n tells me you're a chef. We'll see about that. Grab an apron and a knife. We're gonna skin this stag and throw it over the open fire."

Living in the city, Jordan had never seen a deer and especially never one strung up by its hooves ready to be turned into dinner. This was going to be a crash course in cooking, and Jordan was both nervous and excited. Where else was he going to learn to cook like this?

Jordan watched Mr. Withers start a fire with just flint and knife. He couldn't help but be amazed. "Don't just stand there, boy, grab the pot and fill it with water to hang over the fire." This pot was enormous, almost half the size of Jordan. Jordan lifted the pot onto the hook over the fire next to the deer and began filling it with water. "Now grab the bones and throw them in the pot to give the stew flavor." Jordan would usually just add chicken stock for flavor, but being that he is on an island in a pirate camp, it's not like there is a grocery store where they can shop for things.

Everything that Jordan was making was from scratch. "You ever made deer stew before, boy?" Jordan thought to himself, *I have made beef stew before, so this couldn't be much different.*

"Yeah, umm, a couple times before."

"All right, boy, go ahead and take over. I could use a break. The kitchen's yours tonight. I'll watch, just to make sure you don't go burning the whole place down."

Jordan looked around and thought to himself, *I can do this.* Jordan noticed some tomatoes in the corner growing from a barrel. He grabbed a couple and started to dice them up and threw them in the pot. Next, he noticed a bag of salt and reached his hand in pulled out a handful and threw that in the pot. He began to move about the kitchen as if he had been there his whole life grabbing different ingredients and adding them to the stew.

Mr. Withers watched in amazement as Jordan continued to cook. Jordan took a look at the deer and sliced a piece of meat and took a taste to see if it was cooked enough. It tasted better than any meat he had before. He then cut off a larger slab and placed it on the table and began dicing the meat into small chunks so that they can marinate in the stew and soak up the flavor. Jordan then took a step back, wiped his hands on his towel, and said, "It will be ready in twenty minutes, then we can all eat."

Mr. Withers stood up and went over to the large pot above the fire and dipped his spoon in for a taste. He looked at Jordan.

"This be the *best* stew I've had in my entire life, boy." Jordan couldn't believe what he was hearing.

"Thanks, I have never really cooked for anyone besides myself, so I'm glad that you like it."

Jordan and Mr. Withers began to clean up the kitchen and set the table while the stew marinated.

"Tell me about yourself, boy. What's a clean kid like yourself doing on our island?"

"Well, it's kind of a long story, but a train dropped me off here with just a backpack. The conductor said they will be back in a couple days to get me, so I guess I'm stuck here until then."

"Well, if you're here, then there must be a good reason."

"Mr. Withers, can I ask you a question?"

"Sure, boy, shoot."

"What are you and the rest of the crew doing here?"

"That's probably an even longer story than you ending up here. You see, we came here because we heard that there was buried treasure somewhere on the island. The problem was we only had half a map. The other half was hidden somewhere on the island as well. So we read over the map, and it had a few clues inscribed on the back. We were able to follow those clues, and it led us to the other part of the map. We found the map, but Cap'n noticed there was still a piece missing."

"We searched and searched but still haven't been able to find the other piece of the map. After a few weeks of wandering around the island trying to figure out the map some of the crew started to question, the Cap'n and the crew started to turn on one another. So one night, the captain's brother, Thatcher, took the treasure map, and he and half the crew took off to another part of the island. Now we've been at war with them ever since over a map that is missing a piece."

Just then, Jordan remembered that he had what looked like a piece of a map in his bag. "Excuse me, Mr. Withers, I'll be right back." Jordan left the kitchen and ran to his room. He grabbed his bag and dumped all the contents onto the bed. He looked down and saw the piece of what he could only assume was the missing piece of the map. Jordan ran back to the kitchen, and as he was running, he heard Mr. Withers ring the dinner bell and scream, "Come and get it!" All the other crew were making their way to the table, and Jordan wasn't sure what to do. Jordan wasn't very outspoken, but he knew that he needed to tell Captain he had the missing piece to the map.

CHAPTER 7

DINNER WITH THE PIRATES

Jordan slowed down and made his way to the kitchen. Mr. Withers told Jordan to grab his bowl, and he could pull up the seat next to him. Jordan grabbed his bowl, and as he was leaving the kitchen, the captain walked by.

"Excuse me, Captain Morley. Do you mind if I talk to you for a second?"

"It's gonna have to wait a second 'cause I'm starved. We'll talk after dinner."

"All right. Thanks, Captain."

Once all the crew was seated, Mr. Withers stood up. "Before you go stuffing your faces, I want to let ya know that tonight's dinner was prepared by the new kid, and it's some of the finest cooking I've seen in all my years." The crew all clanged their spoons on the table and were eager to try the stew.

Then Captain Morley jokingly yelled, "Can't be anything worse than what Mr. Withers has been trying to poison us with all these years," as he let out a deep laugh.

"Ha, ha. Very funny." Mr. Withers laughed. "All right. Now dig in."

As the crew started to eat, all you could hear were the sounds of satisfaction with every bite. Captain Morley looked at Jordan and said, "Boy, this is the best meal I've had in all my years at sea. You should be proud of yourself."

"I'm glad that you enjoyed it, Captain."

Jordan waited until the captain was finished with his meal and then asked if he could speak to him for a moment before it gets too late.

"Captain, I think this is important. I was talking with Mr. Withers, and he told me that there is a map with a missing piece that your brother may have." The captain looked at Jordan with a sideways look.

"Yeah, me brother took the map and half me crew. They ran off to another part of the island, and I've been trying to get it back ever since." Jordan reached down into his pocket and pulled out the missing piece of the map. Captain Morley looked at him and his eyes must have doubled in size. "Is that what I think it is, boy?"

"Yes, Captain. I believe it's the last piece of the map that you have been searching for."

In the loudest and roughest voice Jordan has ever heard, Captain Morley yelled, "*Men! Tonight is our lucky night!* Not only is this boy the best chef I have ever had the privilege of meeting, but he also brought us the final piece to the map!" Jordan heard all the cheers of the men, and then all of a sudden, he was hoisted up into the air and carried around like a king. Jordan thought to himself how great is this.

The men were quieted down by the captain. "All right. All right. Calm down. We need to figure out a plan to get the map back from me thieving brother so we can find the treasure." Every time the captain and his crew have tried to take the map back from Thatcher, it has not ended well. As the captain and crew try to come up with a new plan, Mr. Withers spoke up, "Captain, I think I may have another way about going about getting the map back. In the end, Thatcher is still your brother, and we don't want to harm him, right? Instead of going in with guns and swords drawn, why don't we request a sit down? We could tell him that we have found the final piece to the map over a dinner prepared by the boy." Mr. Withers looked at Jordan and winked as if to say you got this. "Maybe he'll forget about the fighting and the stealing and come together and find the treasure like we all intended when we set sail in the beginning."

The captain paused after listening to Mr. Withers's perspective. "All right, that may not be a bad idea especially once he gets a taste for the boy's cooking." Now Jordan started to get a little nervous. It seemed that every time that Jordan cooked, it was under a pressure situation. First, it was for his mom for the first time, then it was for the pirate crew. Now, he's going to cook for brothers who have been feuding over a buried treasure. The captain stood up. "All right. It's been a long night with a lot of interesting events. Y'all get some rest, and we'll plan it out in the morning."

Jordan slowly pushed himself away from the table, stood up, and made his way to his room. He plopped down on the bed and took a deep breath. He took a second and then realized why he was here. Jordan was brought to Pirate Island to help bridge the gap between the brothers and help them find the treasure. The only thing is was how this was supposed to benefit him. Jordan decided to stop thinking and get some rest and not worry about it anymore because he has had the most exhausting day of his entire life. He lay down on his bed and closed his eyes and fell asleep.

The morning light shined through from the slats in the tree house onto Jordan's face. He opened his eyes, took a big stretch, and looked around to see if he was back in his own room, but he was still in the tree house. Jordan thought to himself, *This must not be a dream because it feels so real.* Jordan got out of bed and looked outside and saw the beautiful sunrise. Jordan made his way to the kitchen where he found Mr. Withers. "Aye, boy, good of you to join me." Jordan said good morning and asked if there was anything that he could help with. "Sure. Why don't you grab some of those ostrich eggs and crack them over the pan. We're just going to make eggs and bacon this morning." That sounded great to Jordan since it was simple, and he was going to be preparing a feast for dinner.

Jordan grabbed the eggs, and they were enormous. He had never seen an ostrich egg and wondered if it tasted like a chicken's egg. He cracked the eggs over the pan, and they started to scramble. As Mr. Withers cooked the bacon, Jordan prepared the eggs. Once breakfast was done, they placed the food on the table, and again, Mr. Withers rang the bell. The crew came out from their bunks and sat down. Finally, the Captain came down from his quarters, and they all began to eat.

Breakfast was quiet and then when everyone was done, the captain stood up. "All right, men. Half of you are coming with me, and we're going to head to the other end of the island with our white flags up to talk peacefully with Thatcher. Jordan, you'll be stayin' back with Mr. Withers to prepare the feast for tonight." This was fine with Jordan since he didn't really want to trek through an island to a destination that could lead to two brothers that hate each other and could possibly end up killing each other.

Jordan grabbed his plate, took it into the kitchen, and waited for Mr. Withers in hopes that he would help him with figuring out what to cook tonight. While Jordan was waiting, he decided to look around the kitchen and see what kind of tools, spices, and other cooking necessities were in the kitchen. After a couple of minutes of familiarizing himself with the kitchen a bit more, Mr. Withers came in.

"Got any idea of what you're gonna be cooking tonight, boy?"

"I was actually hoping you could help me with that, sir. Is there a favorite dish that the captain likes? Maybe I could cook that."

"Good idea, boy. Matter of fact, the captain and his brother both fancy mutton and potatoes." Jordan looked at Mr. Withers with a blank stare.

"Uh, what's mutton?"

"It's lamb, boy. Don't ya know nothin?"

Jordan had no clue that mutton was lamb, but he figured it would be something that he shouldn't have a problem with.

Jordan was wondering where they could get a lamb, then out of the corner of his eye, he could see something being tossed his direction. It was an old-fashioned rifle.

"Ever shot a flintlock rifle, boy?"

"Um, I've never shot any weapon before, sir." Mr. Withers smirked a little and laughed.

"Well, you're gonna learn today. I figure we're gonna need two lambs to feed both crews, so let's get out there before it gets too late." Jordan looked at the rifle, and it looked like something he'd seen in a movie and was so nervous because he didn't think that he would be able to kill a lamb. "All right, boy. We'll grab some water and some dried pork and make our way to the north shore of the island because that's where the lambs like to graze. But before we go, I need to make sure you can shoot."

Mr. Withers set up some cans for target practice and had Jordan back up about twenty feet. "All right, boy. You're gonna be shootin' at those cans, so let's see what you got. I want you to take aim at the can, line up the barrel with the can on the left, and once you've lined it up, take a deep breath, and when you exhale, I want you to pull the trigger." Jordan did as Mr. Withers instructed and lined up the barrel, took a deep breath, and when he let the air out, he pulled the trigger. The power of the rifle made him take a step back but then he heard a loud clang. He had hit the can he was aiming for. "Nice shot, boy! Now let's see if you can do it again." Jordan lined up the next can took a deep breath and exhaled and pulled the trigger, and again, he heard a clang sound. He had hit another can. Jordan was so surprised that he was able to hit both the cans on his first try. "All right, boy. You're a natural. Let's grab some extra bullets and head out."

CHAPTER 8

FIRST HUNTING TRIP

As Jordan and Mr. Withers embarked on their journey to the north shore to hunt the sheep, Jordan was starting to wonder if he would be able to kill a sheep when the moment came. Just as Jordan was thinking of this, Mr. Withers started to speak, almost as if he knew that Jordan was afraid.

"Jordan, do you understand the importance of hunting these sheep?"

"I think so. It's so that we can eat."

"That may be true, but it's about much more than that. We hunt so that we can keep a healthy balance in nature. Also, it allows us to become closer to our natural self. Men hunt and gather to survive, and we never kill more than we need as to respect the balance of nature." Jordan never really looked at it that way and understood what Mr. Withers was saying.

"I understand, sir."

"All right, son. It's not too much further to where the sheep usually graze." Jordan was looking around at all the beautiful plants and wildlife that grew on the island and still couldn't believe it was real.

Jordan and Mr. Withers had reached the north shore and found a place where they were going to set up. As they were setting up, Jordan looked around but saw nothing but ocean and open fields. He had never been hunting before, but he kind of figured you might need to see some sign of life in the area to hunt. He assumed that Mr. Withes knew what he was doing.

"Go ahead and lay your cot down behind that bush and lay your rifle down next to it. I'm going to set up behind those shrubs a few yards away."

"What do you want me to do after I set up?"

"Nothing, just lay and wait until you see a lamb and hear my signal."

"What's the signal?" asked Jordan.

"Once we see the lambs, I am going to make this sound." Mr. Withers placed his hands over his mouth and made a bird call that sounded like an owl. "Once you hear that sound, I want you to count to three and take a shot at the closest lamb to you." Jordan nodded his head.

"Okay, I can do that."

Mr. Withers wished Jordan luck and walked over to the other shrub and set up. Jordan looked around and took a deep breath. He lay down on his cot and picked up his gun. He aimed it at the open field and lay there waiting. He hoped that this wasn't going to take too long. While Jordan was waiting he thought about home, and if anyone noticed, he was gone. He thought about his mom and how she was. Also how his friend Nico was doing with basket-ball. Jordan even wondered if Marcus had found someone else to pick on since Jordan was not there. Just as Jordan was about to get a drink of water, he noticed something moving in the distance. Jordan looked a little harder and noticed a flock of sheep.

Jordan grabbed his gun and got ready as the flock moved closer and closer. He waited for Mr. Withers to make the signal. Jordan aimed at the closest sheep to him and tried to picture the can that he was aiming at early. He also tried to remember what Mr. Withers taught him about taking and deep breath before pulling the trigger. Jordan was waiting, and then all of a sudden, he heard the signal. He counted to three, and as he counted, he took a deep breath. And when he got to one, he released his breath and pulled the trigger. Jordan felt his shot go off, and at the same time, he heard Mr. Withers shot ring out as well. Jordan looked up, and he saw that he had hit his target. The rest of the sheep ran off, and Jordan stood up. As he stood up, he saw that Mr Withers was already making his way toward Jordan.

"Nice shot, boy!"

"Thanks, sir."

"Let's string 'em up and haul them back to camp and get them ready for dinner."

Jordan and Mr. Withers finally made it back to camp with the lambs, and Jordan was exhausted. Jordan took a second and looked around, and he noticed the captain and crew were still missing. Jordan completely forgot that the captain was gone on his own mission to get his brother to come back and help him look for the treasure together.

"All right, boy. Why don't you grab a quick nap while I prep the lambs?"

"Are you sure?"

"Yes, you've earned it. Go on. Get out of here."

Jordan went to his room, and when he got there, he looked out the window and saw the beauty of the ocean against the rocks on the beach and the sun shining down on the water. He lay down and recalled the events of the day, how he went hunting for the first time and was able to bring back a lamb that would feed the entire crew. He never thought in his wildest dreams that he could do the tasks that he has completed while here on this island. Jordan was exhausted and quickly fell asleep.

While he was sleeping, Captain Morley and the crew had reached Thatcher's camp. Captain Morley approached the camp with a white flag held up so that they would see that they came in peace. The doors opened up, and Captain Morley and the crew was greeted by his brother.

"To what do I owe the pleasure of the great Captain Morley?" Captain Morley cleared his throat.

"I have some news, and we need to sit down and talk."

"Why should I listen to anything you have to say? You have been nothing but a captain to me, not a brother, or a friend."

"Well this news is bigger than us, so why don't you put that aside, and we can sit down over a meal, and we can reveal the news."

"Why should I trust you? Last week you tried to kill me for the map."

"I understand your hesitation, Thatcher, but I have found the last piece of the map."

"Again why should I trust likes of you?"

"Because, brother, why would I come all this way unarmed to lie to you and risk becoming your prisoner?" Thatcher paused for a moment and thought that what Captain Morley was saying was true.

"All right, Joe. I'll meet you at sunset for dinner, and we'll discuss what you've found."

Captain Morley and his crew left back to camp to let the rest of the crew know that they were fine and that there was no surprises. As the crew headed back to camp, Jordan was just waking up from his nap. Jordan stretched and then looked around. He got up and headed to the kitchen to see what Mr. Withers was up to.

"Hey, boy, you feeling rested and ready to get cookin?"

"I think so," Jordan replied with a little hesitation.

"All right. We'll, it's very similar to what you prepared last night, so don't be stressing and just let your hands and mind connect and do what you do best." Jordan looked at the lamb that was skinned and ready to be cook and thought to himself, *I can do this.* He decided he would make a garlic pepper mutton with mashed potatoes and a mutton gravy and carrots on the side.

Jordan rolled up his sleeves, and he and Mr. Withers placed the lamb meat over the open fire. Jordan then started boiling the water with the bones from the lamb to create the gravy and sauce that he would use for the peppered mutton. Mr. Withers started pealing the potatoes, and Jordan began washing and dicing the potatoes while the sauce simmered and the lamb cooked over the fire. Jordan began to relax and release the tension in his shoulders because he could see the meal coming together like he envisioned.

Just as Jordan relaxed Captain Morley shouted, "Something smells amazing!" which startled Jordan and that's not something you want when dicing carrots. "How's it going in here, boy?"

Jordan replied with confidence, "It is going well, sir."

"Good because things went well with Thatcher, and they will be here at sunset for dinner. And we want to impress him before we get down to business about the map." It was getting late, and sunset was closely approaching, which didn't leave much time.

Mr. Withers piped up, "We will have the best meal you have ever eaten Cap'n." Mr. Withers looked at Jordan with reassurance almost as if to say, "Don't worry, we can do this."

The captain caught a glimpse of the lamb and said, "I can't wait!"

Captain Morley left the kitchen, and Jordan was relieved and could get back to making dinner. Jordan picked up where he left off and began dicing the carrots. Once Jordan finished with the carrots, he put them in the pot to steam alongside the pot of potatoes. Now that the carrots and potatoes were stewing, Jordan could work on the sauce for the lamb. Jordan looked through the kitchen for the ingredients he would need for the sauce. He found the garlic, onions, rosemary, and olive oil. Jordan needed one more thing but couldn't find it in the kitchen.

Jordan asked Mr. Withers, "Do you happen to have any wine?" Mr. Withers reached up on top of one of the shelves and grabbed a large bottle.

"Yep, here is my secret stash. Use as much as you want." Mr. Withers nudged Jordan and whispered, "If you sneak a little for yourself, I won't mind neither."

Jordan laughed a little and said, "No, thanks. I'm not a fan."

Jordan added all the ingredients to the sauce and waited for it to simmer. While the sauce simmered down, Jordan mashed the potatoes and had Mr. Withers take the carrots off the fire and set them aside to rest. Once the potatoes were done, Jordan tasted the sauce, and it was delicious. Everything was ready and just needed to be taken to the table.

CHAPTER 9

BROTHERS RESOLVE

Jordan finished just in time because the sun was setting, and Thatcher and his crew were here. Jordan looked at Mr. Withers and was ready to serve dinner. He and Mr. Withers took the lambs out and placed them on the table next to the large pot of potatoes and plate of carrots. Then he rang the bell for dinner and yelled, "Come and get it!" Both Captain Morley and his crew and Thatcher and his crew sat down, and it was dead silent. Thatcher looked over at Jordan and said, "You must be the new cook." Jordan nodded in silence. Thatcher and the rest of the pirates began to fill their plates with the lamb, potatoes, and carrots all covered in his garlic pepper sauce. Once everyone was done gathering their food, they sat down, and all began to eat. Much like the night before, the men were letting out sounds of satisfaction with every bite. Then Captain Morley spoke up, "Boy, you have a gift. This is even better than the stew from last night!" Jordan was calm and replied with a simple thank you, but inside, he was jumping for joy.

Once the men were done eating, it was time to get down to business. Captain Morley slammed down the piece of the map that Jordan have given to him the night before. He looked up and said, "Men, this is the final piece to the puzzle that we have been searching for! With this piece, we can complete the map and finally find the treasure that we have been looking for." Thatcher stood up slowly. "Brother, I appreciate you coming to me and trying to settle things, and I appreciate you setting up this meal fit for a king. I think you're right! We need to stop this fighting and come together and find this treasure so we'll all be rich." Thatcher rolled out the two other pieces to the map so that the captain could finally place the last piece.

Once the last piece to the map was placed, it showed the path that needed to be taken to reach the treasure. Captain Morley's eyes lit up just as the rest of the crew now that they could finally find the treasure. Captain Morley said, "We leave at first light! So rest up, men, 'cause tomorrow, we uncover our treasure. Before we head off to bed, I think we should all give a cheers to Jordan because without him, none of this would be possible." Jordan was speechless and appreciated the captain for saying that and all the men for recognizing him because back home no one does. All the men stood up and raised a glass and yelled, "To Jordan." And they cheered and laughed for this was one of the best nights for both Jordan and the pirates. "All right, men, off to bed. We have a big day ahead of us."

Jordan walked off to his room, and before he got there, he paused and looked up at the stars and was so thankful for tonight because for once, he got to feel like the quarterback throwing the winning touchdown, and he was soaking it all in. Jordan climbed into his bed and blew out the candle next to his bed and tried to close his eyes and get some rest because tomorrow was going to be another big adventure.

It was first light, and the crew was already up gathering supplies that they may need when on the hunt for the treasure. Jordan jumped out of bed, threw on his shoes, and ran to the kitchen. Mr. Withers was already there working on breakfast.

"Morning, boy. You sleep all right? 'Cause it's gonna be another big day ahead."

"Yes, I slept fine. Is there anything you want me to do?"

"No, I figured after the last couple meals you've made that you deserved a break. I'm just finishing up the last of the bacon, and the eggs are all done, but if you want to help me serve, that will be good."

"Sure, not a problem."

As Jordan was placing the food on the table Mr. Withers rang the bell, and the crew came and sat down for breakfast.

The captain made his way to the head of the table. "Morning, men. Today is the day we've been waiting for. After we finish breakfast, we'll take a second look at the map to see where we're headed." Breakfast was gone in the blink of an eye, and the captain rolled out the map. He and Thatcher plotted out the best path to reach the treasure. Once the route was planned out, they loaded up all the supplies and were ready to head out.

The captain walked over to Jordan and asked, "Would you like to lead the way with me and Thatcher?" Jordan was honored.

"Sure, Captain. That would be amazing."

"Only seems fair since none of us would be here together without you."

The captain and his crew headed out along with Jordan and Thatcher at his side. "All right, men. We're gonna take Blind Man's Pass over the falls then cross at Broken Arrow Ridge, and it looks like the treasure is buried somewhere around the entrance to Claw Tooth Cave. It shouldn't take more than a few hours to get there if we keep a good pace." Jordan got a little nervous because by the sound of all the places the captain was saying the trail was going to be difficult. Jordan was not the most athletic but figured he would give it his best shot.

They had been walking for about a half hour now and had just reached what Jordan could only assume was Blind Man's Pass. It was a narrow bridge that lead over a large mountain form one end to the other and at the bottom was a steep fall onto a rocky river.

Captain Morley leaned over to Jordan and whispered, "Wanna know why they call it Blind Man's Pass?"

Jordan was kind of curious, so he said, "Sure."

"They call it that because it's best to just close your eyes and grab the rope and pray that you make it to the other side." Jordan took a big gulp and looked down over the bridge. He was not so sure he was ready to cross, but if it was to get to the treasure he knew he needed to. Jordan took a deep breath and followed Captain Morley across the bridge. Jordan held on to the rope so tight, he thought his hands were going to bleed. Captain Morley yelled out, "Make sure to not look down, boy. You don't wanna freeze up!" Jordan was not looking anywhere. He took the advice and kept his eyes closed tight and held on to the ropes and prayed he would make it to the other side. Finally, Jordan felt the swaying stop, and the ground harden beneath his feet. He had made it to the other side and was still alive.

Jordan was glad that was over and hoped that it was the worst of it on the way to the treasure, but he had a feeling it was not going to get any easier. Jordan waited with

the captain for the rest of the men to cross. While they were crossing, Jordan noticed an apple tree and decided to grab one to eat while he waited. He sat down with his water and apple. Jordan took a bite, and it was the tastiest apple that he had ever tasted. He decided to grab a couple more and threw them in his bag for later. Now that all the men were passed the bridge safe, they wasted no time at all and continued on the path to the treasure. They walked through what Jordan assumed was the center of the island because it was covered in dense trees and wet marshy fields. Jordan felt like he had been walking forever because the humidity in this part of the island was intense.

Just as Jordan felt like he was going to pass out, there was a clearing. Jordan looked up and saw a steep mountain. Captain Morley spoke up, "Just on the other side of the Broken Arrow Ridge is Claw Tooth Cave. All we have to do is hike over this ridge, and we will have made it, men!" Captain Morley led the way followed behind was Thatcher, Jordan, and the rest of the crew. Jordan was a little relieved because he didn't have to cross another bridge. The hike was a little steep, but they were not moving that fast, so Jordan was able to keep up. They had finally reached the top, and Jordan looked around and this had to be the highest point on the island because Jordan could see for miles in every direction, and it was truly breathtaking.

Captain Morley looked at Jordan. "Quite a view, isn't it, boy?"

"Sure is, Captain. I have never seen anything like this before."

"All right, time to hike down the other side and just about a mile more to the north, and we'll have reached Claw Tooth Cave. Make sure to watch you step, boy. This ground is loose, and if you slip, you could slide all the way down to your death." Jordan made sure every step was with caution because he enjoyed living and wouldn't want to slip and fall to his death.

Jordan and the rest of the crew were slowly making their way down the mountain when all of a sudden, a crew member slipped and started to roll down the mountain, and as he continued to roll down the mountain screaming, one of the other crew members lodged a large tree branch in to the ground, which the crew member rolled into. He had stopped from rolling but was badly injured. This made Jordan even more nervous, and he was extra cautious because he did not want that happening to him. Captain Morley made his way over to the injured crew member.

"Slimy, Baxter, get over here and give Barren a hand. He's gonna need to be carried back to camp."

"Aye aye, sir." The rest of the men kept marching down the hill a little slower after what they just witnessed.

Finally, Captain Morley and Jordan had reached the bottom. The rest of the crew was coming down, and Jordan was getting a drink of water and trying to catch his breath.

Jordan looked around and noticed off in the distance an opening that looked like what he could only assume to be Claw Tooth Cave. Jordan looked over at Captain Morley and Thatcher, and they had pulled out the map and were examining it to see where the treasure was buried. From the look of the map, it was only a few yards away from the entrance to the mountain. "All right, men, grab your shovels and let's make our way to the opening of the cave and be prepared to dig." The men grabbed their shovels and walked over to the cave.

CHAPTER 10

BURIED TREASURE

The men all spread out around the cave and started to dig, including Jordan. They had been digging for around ten minutes, and there was no sign of the treasure. Then all of a sudden, there was a loud thud. One of the men had hit something. All you hear is Captain Morley's voice.

"*Stop*!" The men all stopped. "Who's shovel made that sound?"

One of the men spoke up, "It was I, Captain."

Captain Morley made his way over followed by the rest of the crew. The captain hopped down into the hole and began to dig himself. As he dug, a figure started to become clearer, and it appeared to be a treasure chest. The men's eyes were shining, and their jaws were dropping. "Thatcher, come down and give me a hand."

Thatcher and the captain uncovered the chest and lifted it out of the hole. All the men stared at the chest. The captain looked at Jordan and handed him a long iron bar.

"Here, boy. I want you to bust the lock and open the chest." Jordan looked around, and all the men were nudging him to do it.

"Are you sure, Captain?"

"Yeah, boy. You've earned it. Go on and hit it with everything you've got so we can see what's inside."

Jordan grabbed the bar and held it tight while looking down at the treasure chest. He couldn't believe that Captain Morley wanted him to be the one to open it. Jordan slowly raised his hands and tightened up on the bar. He closed his eyes and swung down with all the force he could muster. A loud clash rang out that echoed over the island. Jordan opened his eyes and looked down. The lock had busted off and was laying on the floor.

Jordan looked at Captain Morley to see if he wanted to open the treasure chest himself. But he looked at Jordan and said, "Go on boy open it and let's see what's in there!" Jordan lay down the iron bar and slowly lifted the lid to the chest. As Jordan lifted the lid, the light from the sun reflected on the gold and jewels inside the chest. The reflection was so bright that Jordan had to squint his eyes. He could not believe what was happening. He had just opened a treasure chest with a bunch of gold and jewels. He could imagine how much this was all worth.

Captain Morley placed his hand on Jordan's shoulder and said, "It's beautiful, ain't it, boy? I want you to know that I am truly thankful for you and bringing me and my brother back together to find this treasure."

"I am glad I could help, Captain."

"Jordan, I want you to remember what you've accomplished here and know that you can do anything and don't let anything stand in your way from getting what you want."

"I will, Captain. And thank you for letting me be part of your crew."

"You are always welcome on my crew boy and don't you forget it." Captain Morley straightened up. "All right, men. We're gonna make camp here on the beach 'cause it's gettin' late, and it is too dangerous to trek back at night."

The crew started setting up tents and getting a fire so they can get something to eat. Jordan started to set up his tent, and he watched one of the other crew members, so he made sure he's doing it right. Finally, Jordan was finished and walked over to find the captain. Captain Morley and Thatcher were sitting down together talking about the treasure and laughing and enjoying each other's company. Jordan thought, *How cool is that?* Two days ago, they were enemies, and now, they are together without a care in the world.

"Excuse me, Captain. I was wondering if there was anything you needed me to do for dinner."

"No, boy. Mr. Withers is just going to pass out the bananas and dried pork that he brought along for everyone."

"Okay, just making sure."

"Jordan, hold on a second. I have something for you." Captain Morley reached down and grabbed something from the treasure chest. "I want you to have this." Captain Morley placed a red ruby diamond in Jordan's hand. "This is one of the most precious stones in that chest, and I want you to have it."

"Sir, I can't take this"

"Jordan, take it and make sure to keep it in your care. You deserve this." Jordan couldn't help himself and threw his hands around Captain Morley.

"Thank you, Captain!" Captain Morley hugged Jordan back.

"All right, boy, don't go makin' an old captain get emotional."

Jordan didn't really spend too much time with his own dad, so for Captain Morley to spend so much time with

Jordan and give him something that was so important to him, Jordan really appreciated it.

"I truly am thankful and will never forget this."

"You are welcome, Jordan. Now go get some rest 'cause we have a long hike back to camp."

"Yes, sir. Good night and thank you for everything."

Jordan went back to his tent and lay down on his cot. He couldn't believe that he had such a crazy few days. He knew in the back of his mind that it was probably time for Mrs. Robinson to pick him back up. It didn't take Jordan long to fall asleep after the insane day he had. While Jordan was sleeping, he could hear a sound. It sounded like a train whistle. The sound was getting stronger and stronger until finally, it was so loud, it woke Jordan up out of his deep sleep.

Jordan got up from his cot and looked out of his tent, and sure enough on the other end of the beach, Jordan saw Mrs. Robinson standing on the side of her train motioning for Jordan to come over. Jordan wondered how none of the other crew had been woken up from the loud whistle. Jordan rubbed his eyes and slapped his face a little to make sure this was not a dream. Sure enough, it was not. It was just like the first time Mrs. Robinson picked him up from his room at home, and he was the only one that could hear the train. Jordan grabbed his backpack and headed over to Mrs. Robinson. Mrs. Robinson looked at Jordan and smiled.

"How was your adventure, Jordan?"

Jordan looked at Mrs. Robinson and replied, "It was crazy! Did you know that I would run into pirates?"

Mrs. Robinson giggled, "I had a feeling that might happen. Why don't you hop on, and you can tell me all about your adventure?"

"Shouldn't I say goodbye?"

"No, I think it's best that we don't wake anyone. It's easier this way. If you want to leave a letter, that would be all right."

"Okay, let me leave a quick letter, and I'll be right back."

Jordan grabbed a pencil and some paper from the train to write a letter to the captain. Jordan thought he should make the letter short and simple. He took a second and thought about what to write. Finally, it came to him. "Dear Captain Morley, I can't thank you enough for everything that you have given me. I wish I could stay longer, but it is time for me to get back to my friends and family back home. Take care. Maybe we will meet again one day. From Jordan." Jordan placed the letter in his tent on the cot.

Jordan headed back to the train and hopped on and made his way to the front where Mrs. Robinson was waiting. Mrs. Robinson looked at Jordan.

"Are you ready to go, Jordan?"

"Yes, ma'am."

"All righty then, have a seat, and I am gonna fire this puppy up, and we'll be on our way."

Jordan took a seat and looked out the window at all the tents on the beach. The roar of the train's engine started, and it started to lift into the air. Then in a matter of seconds, Jordan and Mrs. Robinson were soaring through the night sky. Jordan looked out the window again and could see all of Pirate Island one last time.

Mrs. Robinson yelled back, "So, Jordan, why don't you come up here and tell me about your last couple of days?" Jordan got up and headed to the front with Mrs. Robinson.

"Well, it was all so crazy. After you dropped me off, I was taken by these pirates, and I ended up being their cook. The captain of the pirates was named Joe Morley. Captain Morley and his men were looking for a treasure, but there was a problem because his brother Thatcher had stolen the map, and they were in a big fight after that. I showed Captain Morley the missing piece to the map, which got the two on talking terms. Captain and Thatcher came together for dinner that I prepared to talk about finding the treasure together. They were able to set aside their differences and work together. We went on a hunt for the treasure that was extremely dangerous. We finally found the buried treasure, and Captain Morley even gave me this red diamond from the treasure chest once we found it."

"Wow, Jordan, that sounds like quite the adventure."

"It sure was, and it's something that I will never forget."

"All right, Jordan. Why don't you have a seat? We're gonna be landing back at our destination any minute." Jordan made his way back to his seat and was thinking about how crazy his last couple of days have been. The train slowed down and was coming to a soft landing right outside his house where Mrs. Robinson had picked him up. "All right, Jordan. This is your stop. I hope you had a good time, and I'm sure we'll see each other again soon."

"Thanks, Mrs. Robinson!"

Jordan got off the train and looked around, and it was so weird to be back in front of his house after he was just on an island. Mrs. Robinson smiled at Jordan. "See you in school tomorrow." She started up the train and yelled, "Stand clear," as she began to take off to where ever she needed to be. Jordan took a couple of steps back and waved as Mrs. Robinson flew off into the night.

Jordan made his way back into his house and up to his room as quite as possible so he didn't wake his mom. He took out the red diamond form Captain Morley and placed it on his dresser by the pirate ship in the bottle and climbed into bed. Jordan was so exhausted he didn't even change into his pajamas. The second he hit his bed, he passed out.

CHAPTER 11

Back to Reality

The morning light shinned in into Jordan's room and right onto Jordan's face waking him up. Oddly enough, Jordan felt more rested than he had in a long time. He sat up on the side of his bed and looked down at his feet. He rubbed the crust from his eyes and stretched. Jordan noticed that he was in his pajamas. Jordan then looked at his dresser for the diamond from Captain Morley, and it was right there next to the bottle where he left it. Jordan could not figure out if it was a dream, or it really happened. He figured it would be best not to think about it too much and just try to remember all the cool stuff that he accomplished.

Jordan walked over to his closet to grab something to wear and headed to his bathroom to start his morning routine. He picked up his toothbrush and started to brush his teeth. While he was brushing, he started to put his clothes on, then comb his hair. Once he finished brushing his teeth, he rinsed his mouth with the same mouthwash as always and then headed down the stairs to eat breakfast like he had done a hundred times before.

When Jordan got downstairs, he noticed that his mom was still there, and she hadn't left for work like normal.

"Morning, Jordan. I thought since you made such a wonderful dinner last night, I would make your favorite chocolate chip pancakes."

"Gee, thanks, Mom. That smells great." Jordan couldn't remember that last time that his mom had made him breakfast, but he wasn't going to turn down spending time with his mom. Jordan took a seat at the table, and his mom put a large stack of pancakes in front of him with a tall glass of milk to go with it. "These look great, Mom. Thanks." Jordan took a bite, and the pancakes were great. Jordan's mom took a seat at the table to eat with Jordan.

She looked at Jordan and said, "We're going to have more time to do things like this because I am going to scale back at work so we can spend more time together. Is that something that you would like?" Jordan swallowed his bite.

"That sounds great, Mom. I would really like that."

As Jordan and his mom were eating, there was a sound from the front door. It was Nico. "Morning, Jordan. You ready for school?" Nico walked into the kitchen, and he saw that Jordan and his mom were sitting at the table having breakfast. "Oh, I'm sorry, Mrs. Jenson. I thought Jordan was alone." Jordan's mom smiled.

"It's not a problem, Nico. Would you like some pancakes?"

"Sure, but we're gonna be late for school."

"It's okay. I can drop you boys off today. Go on pull up a seat, and I'll get you a plate."

Nico sat down next to Jordan and whispered, "Hey, man, what's going on?"

Jordan whispered back, “I’ll tell you about it later. It’s kind of a long story.”

Jordan’s mom put some pancakes in front of Nico and then sat back down. All three of them continued eating and chatting about how things were going at school. Once they were done, they placed the dishes in the sink and headed out to the car. Jordan and Nico hopped in the back seat, and Jordan’s mom drove the boys to school.

Once they got to school, the boys jumped out, and as Jordan closed the door, he whispered, “Love you, Mom. Thanks for the breakfast and the ride. I’ll see you after school.”

Jordan’s mom blew him a kiss and said, “Love you too. Have a good day.”

Jordan and Nico walked to their lockers, and while they were walking, Jordan told Nico all about how his parents were getting a divorce, and his mom was going to be spending more time with Jordan and less time at work. Nico put his hand on Jordan’s shoulder and said, “I’m sorry about the divorce, but at least you and your mom can send more time together.”

“Yeah, I guess so.”

“All right, Jordan. I gotta get to class before the bell rings. Have a good day, and I’ll see you at lunch.”

With all that is going on with his mom and dad and the crazy dream that he had last night, he completely forgot about things with Marcus. Now Jordan has to go to PE, and Marcus was going to be there. Jordan headed to the locker room to get changed, and as he walked in, there was Marcus just waiting. Jordan knew he was waiting for him. “What’s up, geek? Don’t think I forgot about you.” And Marcus shoved Jordan into the lockers. Just as Marcus was about to punch Jordan, Mr. Johnson walked in. He looked at Marcus and Jordan.

"Is there a problem here, boys?" Marcus quickly responded.

"No, sir. No problem here." Mr. Johnson looked at Jordan.

"Is there a problem, Jordan?"

Jordan looked at Marcus and then back at Mr. Johnson and said, "No, there's no problem." Mr. Johnson looked at both the boys.

"All right then, finish getting changed and head out to the field. We're gonna be playing soccer today."

Marcus walked out to the field, and Jordan headed to his locker to get changed. While Jordan was changing, he thought about all the experiences he had on Pirate Island. Real or not, Jordan needed to muster up the courage to stand up to Marcus and face that fear that he has always had when it came to confrontation. Once Jordan got dressed, he headed out to the field. He got in his place in line, and they began to stretch. Coach Johnson blew his whistle and then began explaining the goal and rules of soccer. Once he was finished, he divided the class into four teams of seven.

Once the teams were split up, he was glad that he was not on Marcus's team, and his team wasn't the one that he was playing against. For once, things worked out in Jordan's favor. Jordan and his team were playing pretty well together. Jordan wasn't the most athletic, but he was actually able to enjoy himself because he didn't have to worry about Marcus. Jordan was playing offense, and he was even able to score a goal. His team ended up winning, and he was pretty happy about that.

Mr. Johnson blew his whistle, and it was time to clean up and head back to the locker rooms to get ready for his next class. Jordan changed and headed out of the locker room and waited for the bell to ring so that he could head to math. The bell rang, and Jordan walked to math, but he forgot his book, so he headed back to his locker to grab it. On his way to his locker, he noticed Terra was walking in the same direction. Jordan started to walk a little faster in hopes that she would see him and want to say something so he wouldn't have to make the first move. His plan worked. As he walked by Terra, she noticed.

She looked over and said, "Hey, Jordan! Where are you headed?" Jordan looked back as if he didn't know who it was.

"Oh hey, Terra, I'm just headed to my locker to grab my book then off to math with Mr. Horton."

"Oh, I had Mr. Horton last year. He's kinda lame and does that weird snorting thing before he talks." Jordan laughed a little.

"Yeah, that's so weird. He sounds like a pig." Terra giggled a little.

"Well, I have history, and I'm headed that way too. I'll walk with you."

Jordan's face got red, and he said, "Okay, I just need to stop and grab my book real quick."

"Sure no problem."

Jordan and Terra walked to his locker, and while they walked, they chatted about their classes. Terra was at her class, and she said, "All right, I'll see you in science. Maybe we'll get to be partners for another experiment." Jordan blushed again.

"Yeah, that would be fun. See ya later."

Jordan waved and walked away trying to contain his excitement. Jordan got to math and sat down and pulled out his binder and book. Jordan spent most of the class day dreaming about Terra and how he wondered if she was starting to like him even a fraction as much as he liked her. The bell rang and snapped Jordan out of his daydream.

It was time for lunch, so Jordan headed over to his locker where Nico was waiting. Nico yelled, "What's up, man?" Jordan waved back. They started to walk together to the cafeteria and sat down at their normal table. Once they sat down, Jordan told Nico all about what happened with Terra and how they walked to class together. Nico was impressed. "That's awesome, Jordan. I'm proud of you talking to her and not acting like a complete fool." They both laughed and went on eating their lunches and talking about other random things.

The bell rang, and now Jordan was headed to science, which he could not get to fast enough since he was going to see Terra again. He walked in and sat down. Jordan noticed Mrs. Robinson sitting at her desk waiting for class to start. He looked at her, and every moment of last night came flooding back. Jordan thought there was no way that she could operate a flying train. Then he thought about the red diamond that was sitting on his dresser. Just then, Terra walked in, and Jordan forgot about everything again and focused on her.

Jordan waved to Terra, and she smiled back. She came and sat next to Jordan, and he was so surprised because he knew that Terra had a couple of friends in science, but she chose to sit next to him.

"Hey, Jordan, how was math?"

Jordan cleared his throat. "It wasn't too bad, same old boring stuff and more of the pig snorts." They both laughed and the bell rang.

Mrs. Robinson stood up. "All right, class. Today we are going to be writing up our report on the lab we did yesterday making the tornado in a bottle. You will need to get with you partner and discuss why you think mixing the chemicals caused the tornado." Mrs. Robinson put the instructions on the board. Jordan and Terra began going over what they did yesterday. Jordan knew that since Terra was so good at science, this was going to be easy, and they would finish quick. They discussed the previous experiment and wrote down their responses.

Once they were done, they started chatting about things they like to do and what they were interested in. They actually had a lot more in common than Jordan thought. Both Terra and Jordan were born in the same month, they like the same foods, and both were fans of the same football team. Jordan didn't want to tell her that he liked to cook just yet because he didn't know what she would think. As they were getting to know each other, Mrs. Robinson started to speak. "Class, we're going to finish up our responses and turn them in because the bell is going to ring in a couple minutes. Jordan took up their paper and placed it in the basket and went back to gather up his things. The bell rang, and Jordan and Terra walked outside.

"That was fun, Jordan. I'll see you tomorrow."

"Yeah, see you tomorrow."

CHAPTER 12

Jordan's Nightmare

Jordan walked to home economics and could not believe the day he was having and how exponentially greater it was than the day before. He walked in and sat down and remembered that Josh transferred to a new class, so he was going to get a new partner. Jordan hoped it was someone that he would get along with. Just then, the worst possible thing that Jordan could imagine happened. Marcus walked through the door. Jordan wanted to just die. Not only was he going to be in class with Marcus, they were going to be partners. Marcus stood at the front of the class with Mrs. Jasper. The bell rang and then she asked the class to sit down. "Excuse me, everyone. I want to introduce Marcus. He will be joining our class. Marcus, you will be partnered with Jordan at station four."

Marcus looked at Jordan with an evil look, and Jordan sank in his chair. Marcus walked toward Jordan and sat down. Marcus nudged Jordan. "How's it going, nerd? Looks like we're gonna be cooking together for the rest of the year." Jordan closed his eyes and put his head down on his table. When his head was down, he started to think a little bit of his experience on Pirate Island. If he could cook a meal for two brothers that wanted to kill each other, maybe cooking a meal with Marcus might work too.

Mrs. Jasper started to talk, so Jordan lifted his head up from the table. "All right, class. As you know, we are coming to the middle of the year, so today will be your midterm project. I want you and your partner to come up with a dish to prepare and execute for the midterm. I have two VIP tickets to Washington's Culinary Classic for the winner. This is an event where the best chefs from all over the country come to Washington to showcase their talents. "All right, you have two hours to prepare your dish, and I will judge the dishes personally." Mrs. Jasper took a long pause, then she yelled, "*Begin!*"

Marcus looked at Jordan and said, "Oh great, I'm sure that you can only cook grilled cheese." Jordan had enough. He looked at Marcus and gave him a piece of his mind.

"You know what, Marcus? I am actually a really good cook, so if you want to win this competition, you will back off and let me do my thing." Marcus stood there in shock because he did not expect Jordan to talk to him like that. Also, Jordan couldn't believe that he had said that either.

"All right, geek. Let's see what ya got."

Jordan looked at the list of ingredients that they were given to choose from. As he looked over the list, he saw something that popped out to him, and it was lamb chops. Jordan thought to himself, *No one else would use the lamb because it wasn't very common.* Also he had just cooked it for almost fifty pirates so the recipe was fresh in his mind.

"All right, Marcus. I know what I'm going to cook, but to pull this off, we're going to have to put our differences aside. Do you think you can do that?" Marcus nodded his head. "All right. Good. I am going to make a garlic pepper lamb chop with mashed potatoes and carrots on the side."

Marcus looked at Jordan and said, "You sure you can make all that and in under two hours?" Jordan thought if he could make it before in the conditions he was in with the pirates that this time, it would be no problem. Jordan looked at Marcus.

"Yeah, I got this."

Jordan washed his hands and put on his apron and told Marcus to do the same. Jordan walked over and pulled out all the ingredients he needed to make his dish. Marcus just watched as Jordan looked so calm and collected like he had been doing this for ten years. Once Jordan put everything he needed on the counter, he had Marcus come over so he could give him some tasks to complete while Jordan worked on the lamb. "All right, Marcus. I want you to peel and dice the potatoes and carrots. When you are done with that, let me know." Jordan thought to himself how it felt kind of good to tell Marcus what to do. While Marcus was working on the potatoes, Jordan grabbed a pan and put in some olive oil, butter, garlic, and some crushed pepper. He let everything melt together then placed the lamb on the pan. The sound of the sizzle when the lamb hit the pan made Jordan feel like he was back on Pirate Island and everything else just washed away.

Now that Jordan had finished with the lamb, he checked on Marcus. Marcus was done with the potatoes and was finishing up on the carrots.

"Looks good, Marcus."

Marcus looked at Jordan and said, "Thanks," which is something Jordan never would have guessed.

"All right, I'll take it from here. I just need to mash them and add a couple ingredients, then they will be done. If you could take the chopped carrots and place them in the pan with the lamb so they can soak up some flavor."

Marcus grabbed the carrots and said "Aye aye, captain," which was kind of weird because now Jordan was the captain.

Once the potatoes were mashed and the lamb was cooking in the pan, everything was pretty much complete. Jordan rotated the lamb, made sure it was cooking evenly. "All right, Marcus. It looks like were in the homestretch.

Let's clean up and wash the dishes and then we can plate the meal." As Marcus washed the dishes, and Jordan put everything else away, the lamb was just about finished. Jordan grabbed a plate and laid down a healthy serving of mashed potatoes and then placed the lamb right on top. He then poured over the carrots and sauce that the lamb had been cooking in. Everything looked perfect. Jordan added a little parsley on top to make it look fancy and then stepped back to look at his creation. Marcus tapped Jordan on the shoulder and said, "Not bad, Jordan. We may win those tickets after all."

Just then, Mrs. Jasper walked over to their station. "Something smells remarkable," she said. She bent down over the plate to get another whiff. Mrs. Jasper looked up and said, "This is wonderful, boys. I am looking forward to your dish. All right, everyone. Time is up. Come place you dish on the front table, and we will see what everyone has created." All the kids placed their dishes on the table and stepped back. Jordan looked at his plate and then everyone else's. There were a couple of pizzas, one chicken salad, a shrimp Alfredo, and a couple of other dishes that he didn't know what they were. He thought to himself that his dish looked pretty good compared to the other dishes. Marcus whispered to Jordan, "Hey, I think we're gonna win this."

Mrs. Jasper tried all the dishes, and a couple of them she had to choke down. Once she finished, she stood up straight. She looked around the room and said, "Well, there were some pretty good dishes today. One did stand out a little more. Jordan and Marcus lamb is our winner. Congratulations, boys!" Jordan looked at Marcus, and Marcus put his hand up and waited for Jordan to high five him. Jordan couldn't believe it. Jordan gave Marcus a high five and then they went up to get their prizes. Once they collected their prize, the bell rang, and class was over. Jordan put his ticket in his backpack and headed out the door.

CHAPTER 13

RESPECT

Jordan started to walk home thinking about how cool it will be to go to the Culinary Classic. Just then, Jordan felt a nudge on his shoulder. It was Marcus. “Hey, nerd.” Jordan thought, *Well, now class was over, back to normal.* Marcus grabbed something from his backpack, and Jordan flinched because he assumed that Marcus was going to hit him with something. “Hey, I’m not gonna hit you. You can open your eyes. I wanted to give you this.” Jordan looked, and he saw the other ticket for the Culinary Classic.

“Really? You want to give it to me?”

“Yeah, I wanted to say I was sorry about everything and figured this would make up for it. You did a good job in class, and you’re not as bad as I thought, so go on and take it before I change my mind.”

Jordan took the ticket and said, “Thanks.”

“Don’t think too much of it, and I’ll see you tomorrow in class.” Marcus walked off, and Jordan stood there not believing what just happened.

Jordan pinched himself to see if he was dreaming because he could not believe that just happened. Jordan turned around and started to walk home looking down at the ticket still in awe. He thought about how he was able to prepare a meal for two pirates that were in a war, and they came together to work and find the lost treasure. Then the next day, he and his bully were paired together, and the same meal brought them together. *This couldn't be a coincidence*, Jordan thought. His dream had helped him to figure out a way to bridge the gap between him and his bully, just like he did for Captain Morley and Thatcher.

Jordan finally reached his home and opened the door and walked up to his room. He sat down on the bed looking at the tickets and tried to process everything. He thought about cooking and mending things between him and Marcus and the dream if it was a dream, or it was real. Either way, it played a big role in all this. Just then Jordan's mom came through the front door. "Jordan, I'm home!" Jordan got up and placed the tickets on his dresser next to the bottle ship and the diamond. He turned to walk out of the room and took a second look back at the dresser and then closed the door and headed down to see his mom and tell her all about his day.

THE END

ABOUT THE AUTHOR

When Anthony is not writing or working as a social worker, he is spending time with his wife and three sons. Family has always been the center of Anthony's world. Anthony grew up in a small town but always had big dreams of making a difference. With his new series, *Dream Station*, he is able to write about topics that kids may be struggling with but in a fun and exciting way!